T0197408

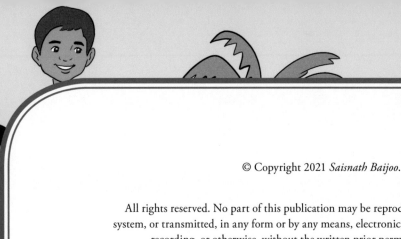

Order this book online at www.trafford.com
or email orders@trafford.com

Most Trafford titles are also available at major online book retailers.

 www.trafford.com

North America & international
toll-free: 844 688 6899 (USA & Canada)
fax: 812 355 4082

Our mission is to efficiently provide the world's finest, most comprehensive book publishing
service, enabling every author to experience success. To find out how to publish your book,
your way, and have it available worldwide, visit us online at www.trafford.com

ISBN: 978-1-6987-0367-1 (sc)
ISBN: 978-1-6987-0366-4 (e)

Library of Congress Control Number: 2021909607

Print information available on the last page.

Trafford rev. 05/11/2021

The adventures of

Spotty
and
Sunny.

Book 6: A Fun Learning Series for kids

Let us have fun at the beach

Author/Pharmacist

SAISNATH BAIJOO

It is a hot summer day as everyone is going to the beach. Dad, Mom, Dominic, Jordi and Cuddles, their dog, are driving in the front in a red car. Close behind in a bright, yellow car are Dad, Grandpa, Jas, and Davin. Jas is taking her white, black, and gray, cute pet rabbit, Bonny, to the beach.

Dad is driving the red car. Grandpa is sitting in the front seat. He plays his guitar and sings along. He sings and claps.

"If you're happy and you are going to the beach. Clap your hands." Everyone claps. He stops his music and ask a question. "Kids, why do we celebrate 4th July as a holiday?"

Jas raises right her hand. She jumps up and down in back seat happy to answer. "I know. I know, Grandpa. It is a special day. We celebrate that our country became a free nation."

"Yes, Jas. One nation, one people, one family united by God." Grandpa says.

Dad says proudly, "Kids, Grandpa served his country as a doctor all over the world. He saved many lives."

Grandpa adds, "Serving my country was a special honor. Kids, maybe one day, this great nation may call you to serve."

Davin interrupts, "Look at those big ships. One day, I want to be a captain of a big ship."

His mom smiles. "Son, you must be a bright boy in school to be a captain."

"Yes, mommy, you know I am your bright boy." Davin smiles as he hugs his mommy.

Mom smiles, "Yes son, you are my bright boy."

Dad says loudly, "Hold on. We are going up a big hill and then down again. Look outside. The sea is beautiful."

"Yes, up and down like rollercoaster rides in Disney parks." Grandpa says holding on to his red, blue, and white hat.

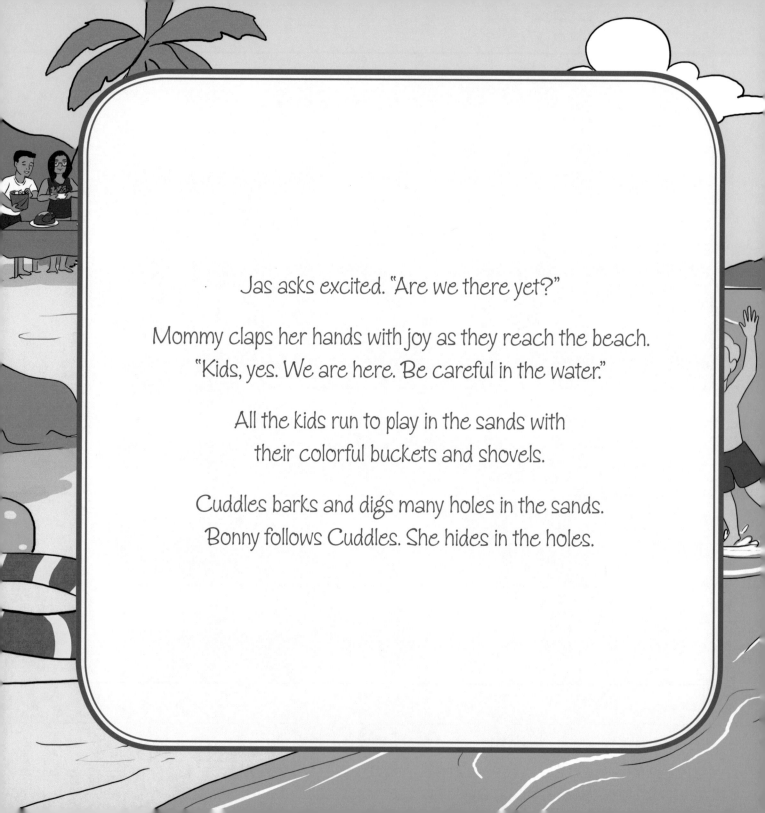

Jas asks excited. "Are we there yet?"

Mommy claps her hands with joy as they reach the beach.
"Kids, yes. We are here. Be careful in the water."

All the kids run to play in the sands with
their colorful buckets and shovels.

Cuddles barks and digs many holes in the sands.
Bonny follows Cuddles. She hides in the holes.

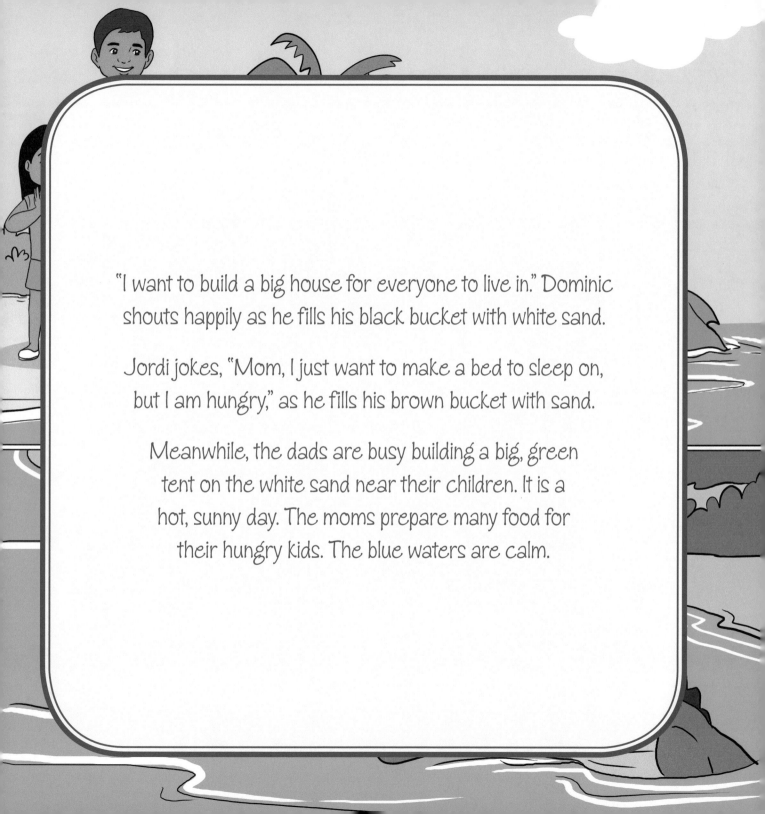

"I want to build a big house for everyone to live in." Dominic shouts happily as he fills his black bucket with white sand.

Jordi jokes, "Mom, I just want to make a bed to sleep on, but I am hungry," as he fills his brown bucket with sand.

Meanwhile, the dads are busy building a big, green tent on the white sand near their children. It is a hot, sunny day. The moms prepare many food for their hungry kids. The blue waters are calm.

Moms sings. "Everyone, come and get your lunch, then, you can go in the waters to bathe."

"But Mom, Grandpa is asleep and snoring." Jas says pointing to Grandpa.

Dad adds quickly. "Yes. My father is tired. He needs his rest." The kids eats their meal in a hurry, then jump into the water. They are happy. Many kids are swimming and jumping in the cool waters.

Suddenly, many playful dolphins swim near the shore. The children are afraid. They run to their parents as many dolphins swim playing near them. There are many baby dolphins and many big ones. They are gray and white in color with white teeth and blue eyes. The baby dolphins dance, sing, and jump in the waters as the bigger one looks proudly on.

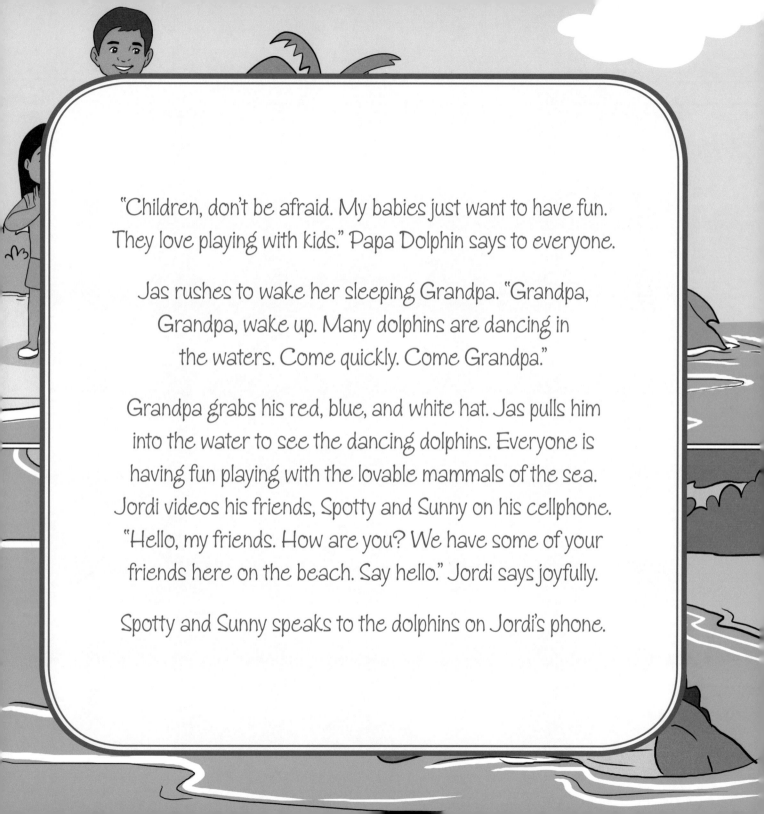

"Children, don't be afraid. My babies just want to have fun. They love playing with kids." Papa Dolphin says to everyone.

Jas rushes to wake her sleeping Grandpa. "Grandpa, Grandpa, wake up. Many dolphins are dancing in the waters. Come quickly. Come Grandpa."

Grandpa grabs his red, blue, and white hat. Jas pulls him into the water to see the dancing dolphins. Everyone is having fun playing with the lovable mammals of the sea. Jordi videos his friends, Spotty and Sunny on his cellphone. "Hello, my friends. How are you? We have some of your friends here on the beach. Say hello." Jordi says joyfully.

Spotty and Sunny speaks to the dolphins on Jordi's phone.

"We are one happy, fun loving family."
Papa Dolphin tells Spotty and Sunny.
Sunny smiles, "Yes, we are. We are one big, happy family."
Jordi says, "Our hearts beat as one. We breathe the same air."

Spotty wonders, "Are you coming to the
Everglades to visit your family soon?"

Mama Dolphin adds quietly, "Yes. Spotty and Sunny. We will
be in there for Christmas holidays to visit our family."

Jordi is happy. "Yes, we will come to the Everglades for Christmas."
Sunny is excited. "Oh yes. Everyone is
welcome in the Everglades anytime."

Papa Dolphin sings loudly, "Family, it is lunch time. Say goodbye
to everyone." The dolphins jump sing and dance as they say a
final goodbye. Baby dolphins cry as they say goodbye. "We love
you all. Goodbye. We will meet again." They swim quickly away.
Everyone is sad as they wave goodbye to the friendly dolphins.

"I am hungry Mama." The children say showing their bellies in fun. Everyone rushes to eat as the moms serve many foods. Dad says, "But first children remember to wash your hands properly."

Grandpa talks about the brave dolphins as they eat their meals. "During the war, dolphins saved many soldiers from drowning when our boats sank." Davin thinks, "They are smart and caring." Dominic jokes, "Can we get a pet dolphin mama?" Everyone laughs. Grandpa adds. "Kids, the fireworks are about to start."

Music plays and fireworks light up the night skies. Everyone claps as many different shapes and colors are made by the fireworks. It was a day of fun at the beach.

Printed in the United States
by Baker & Taylor Publisher Services